Betrayed With A Kiss

A Navy Tale Of Love, Trust, Lies And Deceit

By BF Sanders

Published by BF Sanders

ISBN 978-0-6151-7708-3

This book is dedicated to S Elam. Thank you for teaching me a valuable lesson in love, trust, faith, abandonment, betrayed and lies.

Introduction

I original wrote this book as token of my love for my Sailor. However, I shortly discovered the betrayal, lies and deceit he gave me.

Chapter 1

When I first began to write this book, it wasn't a book about lies and betrayal, but whether a book about Love. However, in the course of writing my book of love poems dedicated to my Navy Sailor, I discovered his deceit and uncovered his lies. As hard as the lesson was for me to learn. The results from the experience of this painful ordeal with this man was a lesson of a lifetime. I hope that my lesson of love, loss, betrayal and abandonment are one that everyone can learn from. As I have learned from it.

It's hard to let things go, but sometimes that is the best thing for a person to do. As painful as it has been. I've been hurt, deceived and betrayed by this man. However, the best thing I can do is to let go and give the hurt over to God. In my process to release this hurt I am able to grow and learn more about myself as a person. Through this experience I am better able to discover in me exactly what is most important to me and my life and how I could use this experience to grow from.

As I move forward in my life I move away from the various childish ways and thoughts of my youth. I look at life now not as a person who has been mistreated and abused, but as a wonderful single woman and mother, who had the courage to stand up and not except mistreatment by others. I also see myself a protector of my child's future as a woman. In taking back my life, I am able to demonstrate to my child, that no matter how hurt I am by the hurt caused by this man I must and have to think about what is most important and keep striving for a better life. What is most important to me is the welfare of my child. It was my intent to let my child see me as strong and not weak in this situation. To see me come out of heart break on top, so when she experiences heart break and pain in the future she will know that life does not have to stop just because of the hurt another person gives to you. For you see you don't have to allow hurt if you chose not to. Just as the various events in ours lives help to grow and learn. They also make us who we are. So if pain comes our way we have to find alternative ways to relieve the pain. Ways that are not conducive to addition pain in our lives, but rather ways to increase a positive outcome in our lives. So if someone damages our heart it does not have to stay damaged.

I'm sure you are dying to know what happened to get me to this place. It's simple a man caused a devastating hurt in my life. How did he do this? I let him into my heart and he stole it, mistreated it, then he ripped it out by deceiving it. This book is about my journal to recovery after that hurt. The story of my ordeal concludes with the book I originally wrote for him. A book love of poems, which were created out the love I felt for him during our relationship.

Chapter2

Ok, I admit it I met him in the worse way possible, online. I had a profile on one of those online sites, were people can email you. I remember receiving his email. It was September of 2006, he wrote me introducing himself as Steven. He said he was in the Navy and would be in the area in a week and wanted to meet me. Well, my answer to him was "no thanks". "I'm not interested in a one night stand". He immediately replied that was not his intention and that I should contact him, because he just wanted to get to know me.

I thought nothing of the email and continued on with my life as normal. However, as the time grew near for him to reach port in my area I toiled with the idea of whether or not to call him. After several days I decided to go ahead and respond to his email and call. He had been in port for several days by the time I decided to call.
 He was both shocked and delighted to hear from me. He asked me to come down to the ship and met him, but I declined. I just wasn't sure of him. I wasn't interested in a one night stand. However, we continued to talk and I grow to enjoy our conversations.

After a couple of weeks of casual conversations he asked me to travel with him to his home town in Longview, Texas. I was to meet his family and friends, but I didn't feel right with doing that. So I decided against it. After all I had just met him. I didn't know him and I just felt as if it were very unsafe for me to go with him. During his time in Texas we enjoyed many long days and nights of conversations, just taking our time getting to know one another. We talked about everything we could. He explained to me that he had a son from a previous relationship. I discuss the problems I was having with the fight for child support with my child's father. We were very compatible and seem to simulate each other.

I didn't know what kind of person he was until it was to late. In the beginning I questioned him about his name. For you see on his cell phone caller ID and on his work email it said one name, which seemed to be a female name. When he explained that the phone and email address were in the name of the person who had the job he was in prior to him and the cell phone was the property of the Navy. I didn't question him. Ok, this is where I am going to stop you from telling me about a bridge you would like to sell me in the middle of the Atlantic Ocean. " no thanks, I ain't buying".

You see I went into our relationship with trust, with faith and ignorant to the devious games of a deceitful man. After all the ultimate hurt is to be betrayed by someone you love. The pain a woman such an experience as I have experience is enough to push you over that edge, but you have to figure out how best protect your heart and make a successful comeback after betrayal.

Chapter 3

The person known to me as Steven Lamar Mitchell and I began a relationship in last September. At the time he identified himself as Steven Lamar Mitchell from Longview, Texas. He told me that he was in the Navy and stationed in Jacksonville, Florida and had one son age 14 from a previous relationship. He also explained that he had custody of the child, because the child's mother had some psychological problems and was seeing a psychologist for her problems. He also informed me that he lived on the Navy ship he in Jacksonville. He never introduced me to the child, because he had sent the child to live with his (Steven's) mother in Texas. During the course of the 15 months of our involvement he deployed out, but continued to develop a relationship with me via phone and email. During the early period of his deployment I experienced a breast cancer scare and since I had no insurance he offered to pay for the surgery to remove the tumor. However, he never, did. He told me that due to the deployment he was unable to move the funds needed. Therefore, I had to begin Alternative Medicine treatments to reduce the tumor.

In June, Steven returned from deployment he indicated that he would return on a date later than the ships actual arrival. When I asked him why he gave me the wrong dates, he stated that he did not return with the ship. That he returned via airplane. He went directly to Texas, because he's mother had been sick and he's son was in Texas. At the time I sent him an email telling him that I believed that his habits had changed in regard to me.

Needless to say, Steven and I decided to make things work. I met up with him in Norfolk, VA for a 4 days vacation. We stayed in Virginia Beach at the Marriott Courtyard and at the Quality Inn in Norfolk near the base.

We continued to develop our relationship. He invited me in August to go to Virginia once again with him in September for two weeks. However, I find that I needed to move from my previous residents to my new home. I was very upset over the move, because it was short notice and I did not have all the funds needed to move. I am a single parent to one child and full time college student with no real family in the area. I was very upset and concerned in regard to the situation. So Steven and I discussed our options. He asked me how much of the funds could I manage to come up with for the move. At that point we as a couple decided that we would attempt to live together. Since he was set to be detached from the ship in Florida to go to Cuba, he assured me that he would be able to travel back and forth between our home and Cuba several times a month. At the time we began to make arrangements for the move, I informed him I could come up with a certain amount towards the move. He agreed to pay the remainder of the funds for the new place which we were going to share together as a couple. However, he continued to come up with excuse after excuse as to why he had not sent the funds. Then in September my brother-in-law, who was a Lt. Commander for the US Coast Guard and a former Navy Officer, was killed in a car accident in Maryland. I was very upset and asked Steven to attend the funeral with me, but he says he would not be able to get time off. Several days after our tentative move in date in September he sent me a small amount of the funds needed via Western Union under what I would later discover was his real name. He told me that he used that name, because he used the internet to send the funds and that was the name on the email address he used. It didn't sound right to me, but I was trying hard to believe and trust in him. He then promised to send the remainder of the money on or before the 21st of September. So I managed to move. Steven claimed that he would move his property into the house and share it with me after he finished one of several classes he claimed to be taking over the summer into the fall months. We were to start building our lives together and planning for our future together. We had plans to open a business together after he retired from the Navy and after I finished all of my degree. However, he did not do as he promised.

I immediately notified Steven of the importance of the funds needed in order to pay bills at the house. Once again he promised to send the money needed to keep the home we were to share afloat, ASAP and I could pay the debts I was incurring due to his promises. He also told me that he would be returning from Virginia and would be bring his belongs to our new home. Then I received a call from him telling me that he was very ill and the Navy was going to grant him an honorable discharge for medical reasons. I asked what was wrong with him, but he could not give me a straight answer as to his illness. This worried me, because we had been sexually involved more than once. After nearly a week I did not hear from him. When I did hear from him he stated that he was in Texas and would be returning to Jacksonville the following week. He needed to go home to see his mother and siblings. Also, he wanted to discuss with them his pending separation from the Navy. Well of course he did not return as promised. I then broke off the relationship with him. Then we talked and he smoothed things over and I asked him what his real intentions towards me and us. He stated that he intended to marry me and grow old with me, but that he had some issues and problems he needed to sort out first, but he would be moving in upon he's return to Florida. Steven then informed me that he would be returning to Jacksonville and after he checked into command he would be on the road with his belongs to our new home. When he got to Jacksonville, I received a call around 4am from him. He told me that command was not going to release him from his duty and he was going onto the water for 5-6 days. Well, during that time I contacted him to share some exciting and good news. He answered his phone and spoke with me of a few moments. Things were fine. After several days I tried to reach him, but I did not receive a reply. So I left several messages. Then on a fall morning I received an email telling me that he would be sending the funds to me and was trying to be faithful to me, but had started to date other women. In reading the email I realize the man must have thought I was a complete fool, because he also told me he was taking his car to his mothers home in order to buy a new truck and even though he was seeing other women he could still live with me. I was like wow.......This is really deep. How could he possible thing that I would stand for such behavior. I guess he believed I would, because I allowed him to walk over me through out the 15 months we shared together, but I am sorry enough is enough. You can only love a person so much. I had to love myself more. In loving myself more, I had to be a good role model to my child. So that she could see the proper way a man should treat a woman. Not a negative way. So as I said I chose to love me.

My response to Steven was:

"Thanks for the email. I appreciate your truthfulness."

Through my faith in God, I was able to clear my mind. I used my thoughts and moments of pray to ask the Lord to show me the way. To show me what I needed to do in order to heal from this hurt. It was as if God had revealed to me a path to express my pain and hurt.

I loved Steven Deeply, so the pain was hard. Shortly after receiving the email from Steven in regard to the other women. I decided to look up the name that was on the email address he gave me. I don't know why I did it, but I did. What I found was that Steven was in deed this other person. So for the entire 15 months of our relationship he was lying to me. Everything he had said to me was a lie. I know men lie, but this is ultimate betrayal. He did not give me the opportunity to make the decision as to whether or not I wanted to be apart of the games he was playing with my heart. Then the plot thickened, I discovered that not only was he lying to me about his name, but he was also married to a woman who was a Sailor just like he was. When I uncovered his marriage I was destroyed inside. My heart went out to his wife, because I could only image the pain he's wife would feel to learn the devastating news of her husband's cheating ways. At that time I had to decide whether or not to contact her with the information. After long hours of prayer and meditation. I made the decision not to break her heart. I decided that I didn't want to ruin someone else's life, because the person they have chosen to live their life with is being dishonest with them. So I decided to leave that situation alone. However, I did contact the Navy to let them know of the deceit, lies and betrayal I suffered at the hands of this man. After reviewing the events of this involvement I realized that this man had abused me. He didn't abuse me physically, but he did abuse me mentally and emotionally.

Chapter 4

The recovery process is hard one, but expressing my feelings in regard to the ending for this involvement has been helpful. My technique used during my time of grief over the loss of love and the plans I had with this man for our future, consisted on attempting to stay positive. I use the principals of Reiki: I will not worry. I will not angry. Nor will I intentionally hurt anyone. I will honor my parents, friends, family and neighbors.

With those principals being a guiding force for me during my heart break. I tried hard to remain at peace and not act out in angry, but rather I seeked advice from others and I turned to God for guidance. The mind is a wonderland and has many ways in order to help combat recovery in a person's soul, because when you have loved and lost it is up to you to turn to your mind to find the answers which lay deep in your soul. Therefore, I had to find a way to silence my mind and find peace during this period of time which caused a great deal of turmoil for me.

In silencing my mind, I was able to see the good in the situation. I was able to see that even through he lied to me in a big way. We shared something special. I will always love him the person I knew not the person he had become. I wish him only the best in life, because as the old saying goes "you reap what you sow". Though it all I will come out ahead and on top of everything. Yet, in my heart there is a pain. A pain of the loss of what was suppose to be. Then again after careful consideration of the events I realize that it wasn't supposed to be. I had to take back my life. After all a woman has to be able to be in control of her life. A life full of joy, love and a sense of being and feeling alive.

Looking back on things I realized for the first time in along time I allowed myself to trust and have faith in someone. I allowed myself to be loved. Even if everything was a lie. I still allowed the feels of love. I sundered my heart to another.

I look forward to the day in which I am ready and willing to try to love, trust and have faith in another man again. Surely, I will receive the blessing in my life of a relationship of truth and honest. As much as I am hurt by this situation I truly care for the feelings of all involved in this situation. I care about my feelings, his wife's feelings and the feelings of the man who deceived me. That is why I chose to let go and forgive him. For you see he worked very hard to achieve his goal. It is my belief that he got caught up in his lie and did not know how to get out of it. So I wish them a happy life. As I continue to strive for the best life possible. I will never forget the journal I walked down during the past 15 months of my life, but instead of dwelling on the hurt, lies, deceit and betrayal I chose to simple move on and forward.

Chapter 5

Prior to the discovery of Steven's lies and other life. I wrote a series of poems to express the love I felt for Steven. He had just proclaimed his love for me. We had begun to plan to start a business together. It was during this time in which Steven stated what his true intentions were toward me. He had planned to marry me, but needed to clear up some issues first. Needless to say, I never thought that the issues he needed to clear up was a fact that he was married and living a lie.

During my hours of sadness, I look back at my reasons for writing this book in the first place. My reasons are clear......love. I was head over hills in love with a man who broke my heart into a million pieces. I had to learn how to pick up those pieces and continue on with my life.

So in reviewing my initial work of a book of poems, which were written prior to the discovery of Steven's secret life, I made the decision to share my experience of love and loss with the world. To share the pain I experience and to share the joy and love I had for this man. I wrote a series of poems on the love I had and the excitement of entering into a promising future of joy I was under the impression would come out of the love I shared with Steven.

I realize that people will make comments that you should have seen the signs and walked away. The comments can go on and on, but my answer is, unless you walked in my shoes you don't have a clue. So don't judge me for loving, trusting and believing in someone. As children we are taught that we must have faith in the unknown and you have to trust, but once you live by those standards as an adult you are convinced to be a fool for doing so. So if I were a fool, because I let someone into my heart then I am a fool.

Please enjoy the poems written out of love, trust, hope and faith I once had in a man who broke my heart. Shortly after the break and discovery of the situation, I read my horoscope which summed up the experience for me in these words. "The way to succeed in life and relationships is to fail and that is ok to move on." You just got to chalk things up as a learning experience.

Night Guide

You are my love
You are my life
You are my guiding light which holds me tight
You are the breath I take at night
As I long to hold you tight
You maybe far away on the sea
But you are always in my sight
For you are my light which guides me at night

Longing

There is no way to express how I feel today

I miss you

I want you

I am waiting for you

I long for the day in which you will be off the sea and with me

Missing You

Missing you by day light

Missing you by the nights sky

As you sail the seas today remember

That somewhere on this great planet of ours

Someone very near and dear to you is missing you

Home

I may not always be able to compose myself the way I would like

But when I'm around you, you bring out the best in me

With you I feel so free

Free to love, free to hold you tight

You make me feel like my dreams have come true

You make me feel so alive and new

With your spirit you charge my soul

So wherever your journeys around the world takes you

Don't forget about the one at home who loves you so

In Your Arms

In your arms I feel new

In your arms I feel rested

In your arms I feel you

Dream Walker

You have brought that feeling of mmmmmmm

Into my world

At night I miss you

I long to hold you tight and kiss you

I long to walk with you on the beach

But since you are on the sea

I will walk with you in my dreams

I love You, Yes I Do

I love your stinky socks

Yes I do

I love the way you hold me tight

Yes I do

I love it when you call my name

Yes I do

And I hope you feel the same

Yes I do

I Miss You

Not many women could live this life

But I am

I am not your average woman

But, what I am is the one who is burning the oil waiting for you to come home soon

I love you Sailor

And I miss you

I Love You Sailor Boy

I never thought I would love such a man

A man who is never home at night

A man who sails the world to protect my rights

But I do, for you see

 I love you

Gentle Kiss

The love I feel inside does not describe the way I feel for you

From now until the end of time

I will love you

I will dream of you

And I long for the day in which you are by my side

The day in which we can cuddle up at night

I long for you're gently kiss

Because you see I miss that kiss

And the way your lips meet mine

I just can't wait to welcome you home with a gentle kiss

Then I will say

"Honey, I'm glad your home to stay

And I hope you missed me too!"

Welcome to the Navy

Welcome to the long lonely nights

Welcome to missing your Sailor

And knowing he misses you too

Welcome to the not knowing where he is

Welcome to trust

Welcome to faith

Welcome to love

Welcome to the Navy life my friend

Blues and Whites

I want to see you in your blues and whites

I want to see you at night

I want to see you with your sailor hat on

For you really turn me on

Hon I Love You and See You Soon

You have my world upside down

I think about you all the time

I miss your face while I'm awake and asleep

I miss your lips so soft and sweet

I miss the way you hold me tight

I miss the way you make me feel at night

I miss our talks, so many there are

And the way you say "hon I love you and see you soon"

Kisses

I love to kiss you

I love the way your Kisses feel to me

I love the way your kisses make me feel

I love the way your kisses make my body burn with pure delight

So hurry home and kiss me tonight

For I love the way your kisses make me feel just right

Navy Uniform

There you are all dressed in your Navy Uniform

So far away from home

But so close to my heart

My heart is longing to see you

All dressed in your Navy Uniform

So when you see me at the end of that dock

Blow me a kiss

Get off that ship and hug me tight

For you make me proud all dressed up in you Navy Uniform

Your Navy Uniform

Your Navy Uniform

Home

Home is where the heart is and yours is with me

My home is with you

You maybe away

But I know we will see each other soon

My heart longs to have you near on cold days

But my heart understands one day you will be home to stay

So remember I am always by your side

I will never leave you

Because my heart is at home where ever you are

Even when I'm not with you

Lonely Nights

Lonely are the nights

So very long and cold without you

As I sit and wait

I wonder if you think of me too

I long to touch your hair

I long to see your stare

I long to hold you tight

But not just for one night

I long to hear your voice

But I know tonight will be just another lonely night

Waiting

As you fight for our country's freedoms

I will wait for you

I miss you

I will wait for you

I will wait for you as you make this land safe and from harm

I will wait as you

Hurry home, because I am waiting for you

When will I see your face

When will I see your face

For you see I want to see your face now

Not just in a picture, but in front of me

I want to kiss your lips

So tell me sailor, when will I see your face

It's been a long time since the last time I saw you

Now I miss you so very much

So I ask you

When will I see your face

When will I kiss your lips

For you see I can't wait much longer

I am exploring within to touch you, feel you, love you

When will I see your face

I love your smile

I love your eyes

I love every inch of your face

But dear one I can't see you

So I have to ask you

When will I see your face

Your face makes me smile with joy

Just the thought of your face near me

Makes me want to jump into the sea

And swim to where you are so you can be close to me

So hurry up and come on home so I can see your face real soon

Our Song

If you were off the sea

I would sing to you

Night and day

Day and night

I would sing to you

I would sing a beautiful song

A song about us

A song to feel the morning sky

A song to reach on so high

A song like no others is what I would sing

If you were off the sea

I wish

How blue do I feel

Everyday I miss you

I want to hear you

But you are so far away from me

I'm missing everything about you

I'm wishing you were here with me

I wish you could hold me tight

Kiss my lips at night

I wish you would hold near

And keep me safe from my fear

My fear of losing you

My fear of not seeing you again

I wish you were here with me

Even if only for a moment

My Dearest Love

I get anger with you from time to time

Because I long to see you face

I long to kiss you lips

No matter how upset I may become it could never change

How I feel inside

Especially when I see your face

So my dearest love please know

I am always by your side

And I will never let you go

I am here for the long haul

My dearest love

Thinking of You

Thinking of you

Day and night

Month by month

Longing for a normal life

I know one day soon

You will be home with me

But until then I will be thinking about you

Until you are here with me

I love you

Alive

The way you caress my body

Makes me tingle with excite

The way you kiss my neck

Make my body come alive

You send electricity throughout my body

From the top of my head to the bottom of my feet

You excite me in everyway

I just can't get you off my mind

Because you make me feel so alive

You would to if it were me

So what

I'm having a bad day

You would to

If I was the one who was away

I stress out night and day

But you would to if I were the one who was away

I cry at the slightest thing

Because I miss your face

I miss the way you snore

You would too if I were the one who was away

I need you

I miss you

And I know you would feel the same if I were the one who was away

Away on the sea

Away from me

I miss you

I need you

Not just because you're away from me

Rather I need you in my life

I need you by myself

To protect me from harm

So it saddens me when you're away from home

I miss you

I need you

I want to hold you tight

Not just because you're away

But because I love you with all my might

Remembering

As I go through my day

I remember you

I remember us

I think back on when we meet

And I smile

I never want to forgot the first time I saw your face

I never want to forget the way your eyes meet mine

I just want to remember for all times

As I go on my day I will remember the way I feel inside

I feel grateful and sure

I feel secure and new

I feel loved and that's for sure

So I will remember your smile

I'll remember your love

I'll remember the way you make me feel

I will long to hold you near

I will wait patiently to look upon your face

I will wait to hold you near

I will hold you in my heart for all time

For you see I love you with all my might

When you come home I will be here waiting for you and longing to hold you near

Comfort you and keep you warm

As we sit back and remember the very first time we glanced into each others eyes

Thank You

Thank you for being in my life

Thank you for being so kind

Thank you for showing me the way

The way to love again

Thank you for holding tight to me

Through our ups and downs you just won't let me depart

Thank you for being the man I need

I love you

I love you

I love you

Proud

I hate waking up in the morning without you near

I hate going through my day without you

I hate not knowing when you will be home

But I am so proud of you

I am proud that you are protecting me

You are protecting my rights

You are protecting our children

You are protecting our nation

So if from time to time you think I don't understand

I do

It's just that I miss you

Raining

The rain hides my eyes

The rain hides my tears which I feel inside

As I long for you each day

There are a few things I want to say

I need you

I want you

I love you

The rain comes and goes

So do my tears on the outside

But I will always cry on the inside until you come home

The Candle and Flame

As we grow

 I must let you know

I care for you

As you go away to sea

I want to know

I care for you

You are my candle

And I am your flame

Together we glow

And light our path

Even as you're away from me

We are glowing together and lighting the way

So as you come closer to home

Look out on the horizon my love

And look for your flame

For I am here for you my candle love

As we reunite so does our love

A love we hold so shiny and new

A love like no other

A love that can stand the test of time

A love for all eternity

A love of a flame and a candle

A love that will burn for a lifetime

I love you and will also be here

I love you and will also be here

I'm here for you

Through good and bad times

I would never turn my back on you

It is sometimes very hard to be in this life

A life were your deployment keeps you away from me

Sometimes I get very angry with you

But I would never abandon you

I'm here for the long haul you see

I'm here for life

I love you and will always be here

Garden

You are the seed in my garden

I hold you in me so deep

We grow together

Feet by feet

As we grow our branches extend

Up and up they go as we grow

Our flowers bloom

As our bodies entwine into one

As we grow apart we also grow together

Reaching, growing, loving

I reach for your hand you reach for mine

As we hold each other tight in our entwine

We stand together strong and true

I am proud to be with you

You're my tree and my rock

I hold you near

As we become a earthly and heavenly pair

Trees

We are reaching for the sky

 We are reaching up high

As we grow we know each others love grows

Our branches keep each other warm

We started together as nothing, but a mere seed

Now look at how tall we have become

From just a little seed

We grow with love

For we are the tree which brings about life to our future

From our growth together we will create forever

As our seeds fall from our leaves and grow into other trees

Our Light

Our light is shining bright

It leads you home

As you fight for our rights

Our light leads you home

As you cross the sea

Our light leads you home

When you're away from me

Our light leads you home

Stars

At night when you are on the sea

Do you miss me

I miss you at night when you're away from me

When I need to hold you close to me

I go outside and look at the night sky

For I know where you are deep inside of me

We will always be together

As we glance at the stars in the night sky

As you can hold me tight

I feel your lips carefully kissing mine

We will hold each other close

Even when we are far apart

Just by looking up to the stars at night

The stars will guide you back home to me

The stars are so gentle you see

So whenever you are missing me

Look up at the stars

And just be

Just be happy in knowing that

I am holding you tight

I am kissing right

Especially at night

Proud of You

I am so Proud of You

Have I ever told you how proud I am of you

You honor our country

You protect me too

You fight for our rights

You are a very special man

A warm caring man

A loving man you are

I am so proud to be in your life

I am so proud to be your love

Wherever your career leads you

Please know I will follow you

And I will keep our house and family safe

As you protect us day by day

I am so proud you

Prayer

Dear Lord,

Bring my Sailor home to me

I missing him each and everyday

I try not to cry when I talk to him

But Lord missing him is sometimes to hard to bare

I want to see his face

I want to hold his hand

I want to kiss his lips

Lord don't you understand

As proud of him as I am

I know it maybe selfish of me

But I need him

I want him

I miss him

I don't want to go to bed without him

I don't want to awake up alone

But if that is your will Lord

I will wait for him to come home

I will wait as long as it takes until he is here with me

I ask you Lord keep him safe from harm

Bring him home to me

So I can spoil him with my charms

I can show him how much I love him

We'll cuddle

We'll walk in the park

We'll talk

I know it's a lot to ask

But I truly miss him so

I know he will be home as soon as he can

I really miss him so

Lord I just need him to know

I need him to know how important he is to me in every way

So please lord hold him tight and keep him safe from harm

And bring him home right away

Also watch over all our troops

Bring them home safe from harm, to those who love them the most

Lord, please take extra care of my Sailor and bring him home

For you see I long to walk with him

Laugh with him

Love him

Amen

Yours

No, I won't abandon you

You're away to sea

While I am here all safe as can be

Although you are far away from me

You are right in the center of my heart

You never have to worry about me straying away from you

For you see I'm yours everyday

Everyday I wait for you

I wait for you to hold me near

I'm yours forever

I'm yours for all times

I would never leave you

All I want to do is stay by your side

You stole me heart and I don't want it back

I want you to keep it

Love it

Know in your soul my heart is yours

It could never belong to another

Old Fogies

From the first time I heard your voice I knew

You were the one I wanted to share my life with

You are the one I want to grow old with

I want to watch your hair turn white

I want to laugh with you at night

I want to talk with you

Sing with you

And love you too

As we hold hands and share in our old rocking chairs

Share stories of the past

Share stories about our life together

I look forward to our old age together

As we take care of one another

As we watch our children and grandchild grow and learn

We will laugh as they laugh at us for being those old fogies in the rocking chairs

Worry Wart

It can be hard for me to acknowledge that I am a worry wart

I try and try again to stop my worry about you dear man

But it's hard you see

For my love for you makes me so weak

All I want to do is make sure that you are happy too

Just like I am with you

So forgive me of my faults

Except me for imperfections

And know that I am trying as hard as I can

To stop being such a worry wart dear man

Do you still love me

As I wake from my slumber

I wonder

Do you still love the same as you once did

I cry at night as I wait for just a call or a letter

It seems like it's been far too long since you were last here

Here with me wherever I am

Wanting you

Need you

Missing you man

So as I sit here waiting to hear from you

I will just write

I hope you come home soon

10 Long Days

I miss hearing your voice

There have been other times when you've been away

But this time it's just not the same

I haven't hear from you

I know your working

But I'm really missing you

It's been 10 long days

10 long days and no contact from you

Not an email not a phone call

Want do I do

As I sit and wait to hear your voice

I just want you to know

I miss you of course

Come Back to Me

I miss the way you hold me

I miss your smile

I miss the way you listen to me everyday

Come back home my friend come back home to stay

See you're just my man

You are my best friend

And when you are away like this it just kills me to no end

It kills me deep inside not to be able to hear your voice again

And not to be able to touch your lips of course

Come back soon

Come back to me

Until we meet again my friend, my man

I know this is not the end

Can't Sleep

I can't sleep tonight thinking about you

Wishing you were home, you see

Wishing that there was no war

Long to hold you so

Long to hear you whisper in my ear

Good morning hon

Which would make my scream

Scream for delight

Scream at night

Knowing your home

And I don't have to worry anymore

My Heart Hurts

My heart hurts so because it longs for you

I long to see you

I can't bare this pain I feel when you're not here

It hurts me so deep inside

But who is to blame

Who is to blame for the pain I feel

No one is to blame but Cupid himself

He stole my heart to give to you

You've had my heart since day one

And you'll have my heart until the day we both depart

When I depart from this earth

Please know dear Sailor how truly blessed I would have been

Bless to know your name

Bless to love you

Bless to know that you love me to

So yes my heart hurts and longs for you

But I know that soon it will be with you

Forever and ever it will

As we grow old together

Walking hand in hand

I Hate Your Cell Phone

I hate your cell phone

When I call why don't you pick up

It drives me crazy

Because when you call me I always pick up

What is it about men and these phones

You want me to call

Well pick up man

Pick the phone up

And hurry home

It could be an emergency

What happen to my call

Did it get lost in cyberspace

Whatever the problem just pick up the phone and holler

Let me know your ok

I Want My Man Home

You see it takes an extra special woman to live this life

A life like this is very hard you see

For all I want is you here with me

I want my man home

I don't want to handle life alone

The bills, the household repairs

Those are just a few things for us to share

Long passionate nights

Walks on the beach

Hurry home and see about me

It hurts me so to watch other couples together

When I know I'm missing my better half

So hurry home my love

So we can walk together

Talk together

And just act like crazy fools

Cool Summer Day

Do you remember that cool June day

When we sat and did nothing all day

We sat and enjoyed life

We enjoyed one another

We listened

We watched

We laughed

And we smiled

I long for those days to be many

It's just the waiting can be such a killing

It's hard to miss the one you love

Long for you to hold me and keep me warm

Until you come home I will sit back and remember that cool summer's day way back in June

Description of the Perfect Man

If I had to describe you

I would start off by describing your eyes

So warm and sincere

So tender and kind

Especially when I'm near

Then I would describe the nose on your face

As just as sweet as the rest of your face

Your lips I would say are warm and inviting

Just the kind I long to kiss at night

Your body so protective and strong

You are perfect to me in everyway

Navy Significant Others Need a Medal

It's hard to live as a Navy Significant Other

You have to learn to trust

And learn to trust on the double

So many nights I get mad with frustration

That I can hear your voice or see your face

Your fight maybe on the physical level

By my fight is on an emotional level

I fight day and night with my feelings and emotions of missing you

I fight with the running of our life without you here

It's hard and I say today

Just like you I need a medal

If I received a medal it such read

This medal is for The Navy Significant Other of the year

www.ingramcontent.com/pod-product-compliance
Lightning Source LLC
Chambersburg PA
CBHW050311260626
47156CB00005B/1757